A
WALK
in the
WORDS

BY HUDSON TALBOTT

⊙ NANCY PAULSEN BOOKS

For Charlotte Sheedy,
with love, respect,
and gratitude

NANCY PAULSEN BOOKS
An imprint of Penguin Random House LLC, New York

Copyright © 2021 by Hudson Talbott

Nancy Paulsen Books is a trademark of Penguin Random House LLC.

Visit us online at penguinrandomhouse.com

Library of Congress Cataloging-in-Publication Data is available.

Manufactured in China by RR Donnelley Asia Printing Solutions Ltd.
ISBN 9780399548710
3 5 7 9 10 8 6 4

Design by Nicole Rheingans. Conceptual design by Hudson Talbott.
Text set in Grota Sans Alt Rounded.
The art was done in watercolors, colored pencil,
and ink on Arches watercolor paper.

This is a work of nonfiction.
Some names and identifying details have been changed.

Robby's
Aunt Opal

Get off my lawn!

HEY!

her dog Poopy

Drawing always came naturally to me.
I drew all the time. I just did it,
like breathing.

Every day, after playing with my friends,
I'd come home and draw stories that I made up.
It was like diving into my own world.

I liked words, too—one at a time.
When I was reading,
I had to picture every single WORD.

But long sentences? No way!

began to wander.

I would start a long sentence and then my mind

I was the slowest reader in my class.
When everybody was turning to the next page,
I was still on the first sentence. Nobody knew.

But the books knew!

And they were coming for me!
So many words! So many pages!

Books weren't always scary.
The first ones were friendly, with
big pictures and only a few words.

But little by little,
the pictures got smaller
and the text got longer.

I could pick out the words that I knew but the rest looked like squiggles

It was a rain of terror.
My drawing pad was my safe place.

A whole page of text looked like a wall—keeping me out.

Thomas Hart-Henry Clay house at Lexington is an example of the Greek Revival style.

Religion. Episcopalians held the first church services in Kentucky in 1775. Three Baptist churches had been established in the state by 1781. Many churches were founded during a period called the Great Revival which swept Kentucky in 1820. This revival spirit attracted a religious group called the Shakers, who established a colony at Shakertown (now Pleasant Hill).

The Baptists are the largest religious group of present-day Kentucky. Other important religious groups are the

houses made of square logs from
s had been cut. Stone houses ap-
ere built in the Georgian, Federal,
Gothic Revival styles of architec-
ouse, near Bardstown, was built in
mes called "The Home of Three
d for its fine carved doorways and
John Rowan's "Federal Hill," a
orgian home, is also located near
ry Massey House, built in 1804 in
building in the Federal style with
lightly carved woodwork. The

in Hawaii. If the seismographs on Hawaii and at other places show that a quake has occurred off the Aleutians, the forecaster figures the minutes that it took the earth tremor to reach the seismograph. Then he figures that it will take about the same number of hours for the wave to hit the islands. The basis for this system of forecasting tidal waves is that quake tremors travel from 350 miles or more a minute, while water waves travel in accordance with the depth of the water. In the open sea this is at the rate of 400 to 500 miles an hour.

A tidal wave fifty feet high wrecked Lisbon, Portu-

is also ground and treated chemical
called *wet milling*. The principal proc
are starch, livestock feed, and oil. W
very careful control, large manufact
machinery and equipment, and a
chemists, and other skilled technici-
using ever-increasing amounts of co
ample, almost 62,000,000 bushels
1942 the amount was more than do
rising.

Cornstarch from wet milling is

> **By now, everyone in my class was reading book after book, except me.**

laden waters dissolved iron out of rocks with which they came in contact. These iron-bearing waters flowed into the oceans. Here the iron slowly fell to the bottom. Great beds of iron oxide, sand, and silt drifted in piles hundreds of feet thick on the ocean bottom. Heat and pressure formed these beds into rock.

Later, earthquakes and the shrinking of the earth's crust brought these rocks to the level of the water. Here other changes occurred. Great glaciers, thousands of feet thick, moved down from the north. These moving ice sheets gouged and tore at the rocks and sediments

places, waters seeping through the rock have dissolved out much of the worthless sand, leaving the iron ore behind.

This is just one method by which iron ores of usable quantities were formed. In some areas, the slow cooling of molten volcanic rocks produced iron-ore deposits. In other areas, the action of tiny organisms living in the water caused, and is still causing, iron oxide to form.

Kinds of Iron Ore. Ores are a mixture of minerals. Some ores are rich in iron. Others are less rich and have

Townsend (*Lincoln and His Wife's Home Town*), J. Winston Coleman, Jr. (*Stage Coach Days in the Blue-Grass* and *Slavery Times in Kentucky*), and A. M. Stickles (*Simon Bolivar Buckner, Borderland Knight*). Others include James Lane Allen (*A Kentucky Cardinal*), Elizabeth Madox Roberts (*The Time of Man*), Ben Lucien Burman (*Steamboat Round the Bend*), and Jesse Stuart (*Beyond Dark Hills*). The Americans are indebted to Kentucky for the humor of Irvin S. Cobb and that of Alice Hegan Rice, author of *Mrs. Wiggs of the Cabbage Patch*. Madison Cawein and Cale Young Rice are among the famous

a large number of impurities, such
phosphorus, silica, and sometimes ti
pal ores from which iron is pro
minerals hematite, limonite, magne
Hematite usually occurs as a red-
is the source of about 85 per cent o
in the United States. In its pure for
tenths iron. See HEMATITE.
Limonite is a yellow-brown mine
of only about 1 per cent of the iron
States. See LIMONITE.

d in goods. For example, a man
y agree to pay his landlord a cer-
as rent.
in certain items of information if it
ct. These include the names of the
dates of the beginning and end of
of rent, a complete description of
mplete statement of the rights and
Most state laws provide that leases
ess than a year need not be written,
period must be in writing. R.F.B.

if the fireplace is put at one side or corner of the room and provided with a chimney, the smoke will pass up the chimney. The addition of the chimney also provides a draft by which the air enters the front of the fireplace and passes up the chimney to increase the burning. In some modern fireplaces open ducts have been put below the fireplace to take in cold air from the floor of the room and other ducts are placed at the sides of the fireplace. These give off warm air and further heat the room.

But fireplaces must be located on one side wall or in a corner of the room. This limits the area to which they

TIDAL WAVE. Sometimes great waves sweep in from the ocean like a huge tide, and destroy everything in their path. Most persons call these *tidal waves*. But the term is rather misleading, because tidal waves are not connected with true tides, which are governed by the sun and the moon and come at definite times.

Destructive tidal waves are caused by undersea earthquakes, called seaquakes, or by hurricanes far out to sea. It is possible to tell almost the exact time that a tidal wave will occur from a distant earthquake by the use of seismographs. Scientists know by observation that earthquakes off the Aleutians

gas-st
steam
duce
large
of the
heati
can b
Loc
room
source
heat

Kentucky began in 1911, and is active today.

Lexington in 1825 was a center for such portrait painters as Matthew H. Jouett, who was called "the best portrait painter west of the Appalachians" by the people of his time. John James Audubon studied the bird life of Kentucky at Henderson and Louisville from 1810 to 1819, and completed many of his paintings for his world-famous *Birds of America*. Frank Duveneck became a leading American painter, etcher, and sculptor during the 1850's.

Kentucky is especially noted for its folklore and folk

corn. The whole grains are also tre
washed carefully and served as white
as hominy. But we eat a far great
foods that are manufactured from t
The seeds are ground to powder, fo
corn meal. This we use in bread, cak
griddlecakes, mush, scrapple, hot tam
dozens of other foods. Meal that is
made into hominy grits. The grits m
are rolled out flat, after flavoring wi
other things, to make corn flakes. M
are also used in the manufacture of b

> **What if they found out that I couldn't keep up?**

ing and further grinding until it is
ur. Corn flour, which looks some-
h, is used in baking and sausage
ake flours have a little corn flour

nery in a "cured" form, which means that they have been treated to prevent their rotting before they reach the tannery. The hides and skins are immediately soaked in water to soften them and to remove any substance which has been used as a curing or preserving agent. The soaking period varies from two to forty-eight hours, depending upon the condition of the hide. After the soaking

Central heating is more common in the United States than in any other country. But local heating is still in common use in many countries.

The earliest type of local heating system was the open fire in an enclosure such as a cave or a tent. This method is still used among many primitive peoples in the world, and was often used by the American Indians

M
gas-
chan
with
provi
furna
The e

I had to face it:

I was alone and lost in a world of . . .

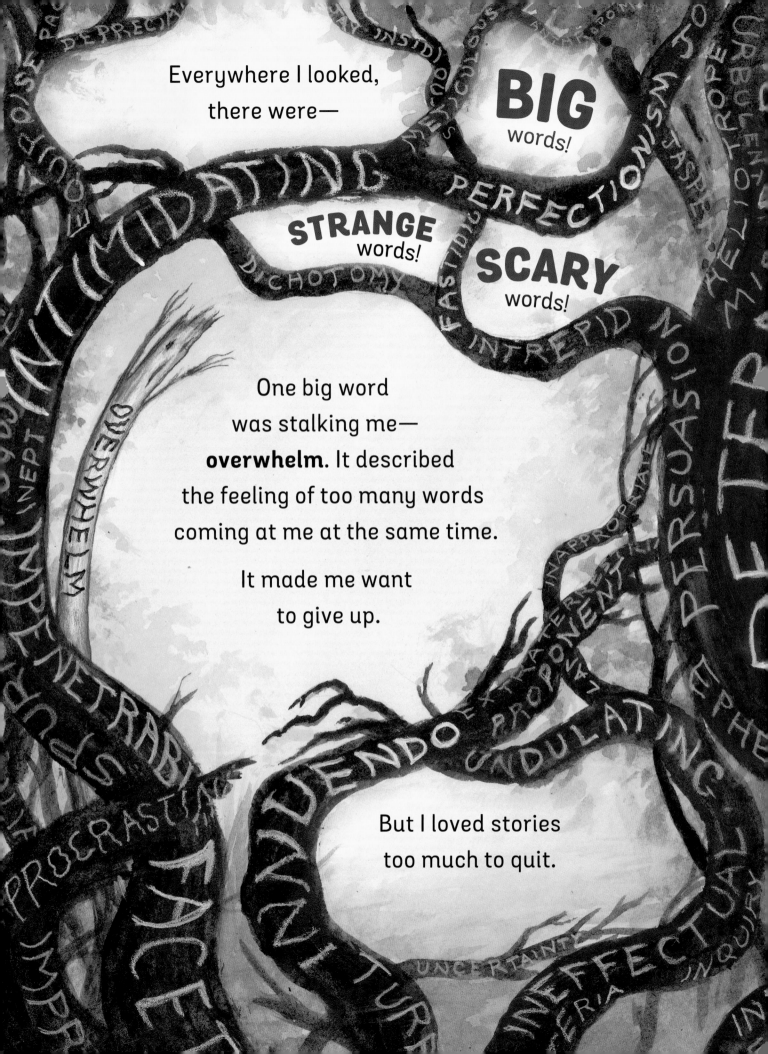

Everywhere I looked,
there were—

BIG
words!

STRANGE
words!

SCARY
words!

One big word
was stalking me—
overwhelm. It described
the feeling of too many words
coming at me at the same time.

It made me want
to give up.

But I loved stories
too much to quit.

I was good
at picturing stuff.
Maybe I could try
picturing a way out.

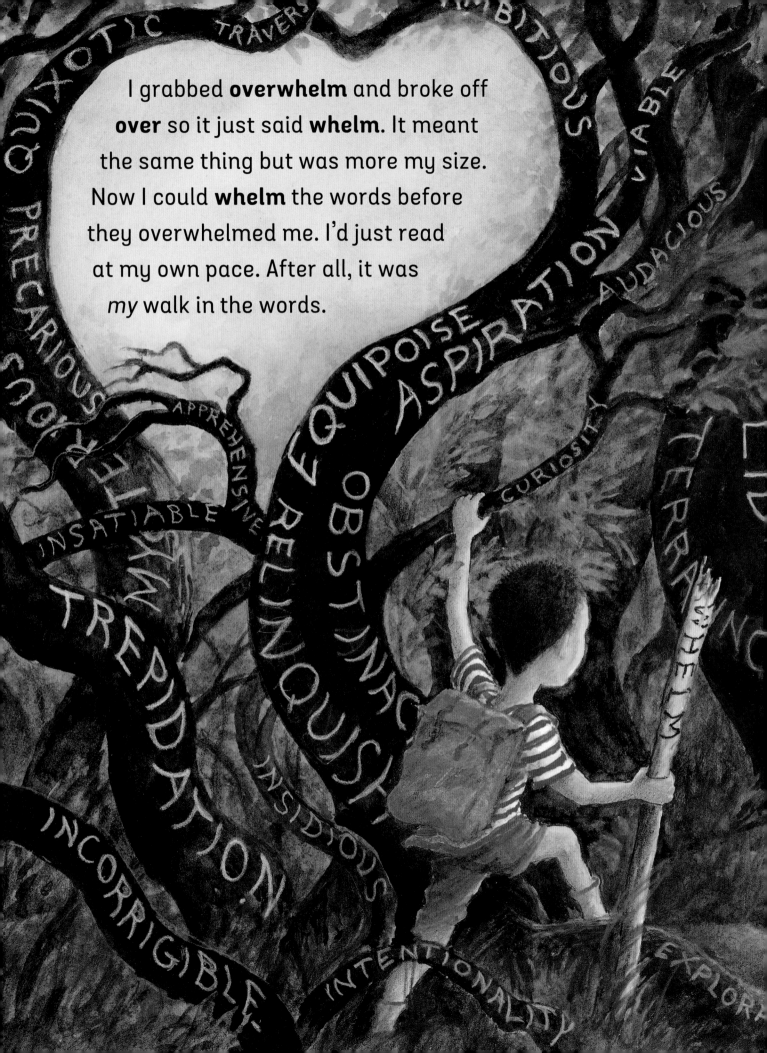

I grabbed **overwhelm** and broke off **over** so it just said **whelm**. It meant the same thing but was more my size. Now I could **whelm** the words before they overwhelmed me. I'd just read at my own pace. After all, it was *my* walk in the words.

I took time to look
for words that I knew.

There they were!

Like stepping-stones
leading me onward.

I jumped over the words
I didn't know,

and let the words
I knew lead me into the story.

After a while, I wasn't thinking about reading.
I just wanted to know what happened next.

we come in peace

The war between my fear of reading
and my curiosity was over.
Curiosity won.

YEE-HAAA!

Books weren't so scary,
once I got to know them.

And now that I was
beginning to like words,
why rush past them?

READ
AT YOUR OWN
SPEED

I realized that just because I was slow
at reading didn't mean that I had to fear it.
I also learned that many great people
were slow readers.

I honored them all in my . . .

And I tore down that terrible . . .

WALL OF SHAME

Slow readers savor the story!

I experimented with ways to tell my stories.
I could still tell a story with pictures.

Or I could tell it with words.

The Monster from Planet Mungo
Chapter 18

The monster cornered me.
My gun jammed! I had to think
fast or Earth was doomed!

My favorite way was using both.

I remembered how my horses got better
the more I drew them. My writing would
improve too, if I wrote every day.

A drawing could show what a horse looked like.
But with words, I could bring them to life.
Now they could breathe and snort
and carry me on adventures.

I read every day, in search of new words
for my stories. It was like finding
new colors for my art, but now
I was learning to paint with words.

There were still times when I felt lost in a sea of words. My drawing pad was still my safe place. Others found music, sports, math, and science.

Words had always scared me. But once I felt free to read at my own speed, they became my friends. I could unlock the magic of stories and even become a storyteller myself, turning that sea of words into an ocean of possibilities.

Only after school, I'd come home and draw stories... I took til[e]... words I could say how it felt... at our own pace... My drawing pad was...

in the flow... After all it... My... it was like diving into my...

I liked words... ew words gave me options for telling stories... I could paint with words... too - one at a time... but others found their s...

Art rescued me... but others... read at your own pace... your own speed... STORY

okay to go at my own... and my fear of reading... e war between my... and my curiosity was over. Curiosity won. whelm the words before

Now all I have to do is
enjoy the ride!